Before reading this book to know:

· Sounds can be spelled by more than one letter.
· The spelling ‹ur› represents the sound /er/.

This book introduces:

· The spelling ‹ur› for the sound /er/.

Words the reader may need help with:

is, my, says, me, have, give, you're, hurled, his, to

Vocabulary:

have a turn – have a go
hurl – to throw

Talk about the story:

Have you ever played with a friend who will
not let you have a turn playing with his toy?
Burt won't let Frank have a turn.
Frank gets upset. Will they stay friends?

Reading Practice

Practice blending these sounds into words:

Burt

turn

hurls

hurts

curls

burn

surf

nurse

My Turn

Burt is on a hopper.

"It's my turn," says Frank.

"Burt, let me have a turn!"

says Frank. "It's my turn!"

Burt will not give Frank a turn.

"You're not my pal!" says Frank.

Then Burt is hurled off. His
leg hurts. His hand hurts.

He curls up and hugs himself.

Frank runs to help him.

"Burt, my mom can help!"

"Thanks, pal!" says Burt.

Questions for discussion:

- Why doesn't Burt let Frank have a turn on the hopper?

- How does Frank feel about it?

- Do you think Frank should help Burt?

Game with <ur> words

Play as 'Concentration' or use for reading practice. Enlarge and
photocopy the page twice on two different colors of card.
Cut the cards up to play.
Ensure the players sound out the words.

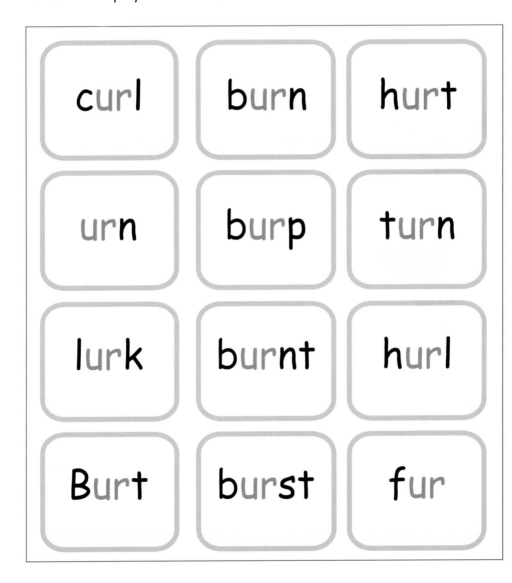

curl	burn	hurt
urn	burp	turn
lurk	burnt	hurl
Burt	burst	fur